One Night in the Zoo

For Ian Craig
who made this book possible,
with love and thanks

Picture books by Judith Kerr

The Tiger Who Came to Tea

Mog the Forgetful Cat

Mog's Christmas

Mog and the Baby

Mog in the Dark

Mog's Amazing Birthday Caper

Mog and Bunny

Mog and Barnaby

Mog on Fox Night

Mog and the Granny

Mog and the V.E.T.

Mog's Bad Thing

Goodbye Mog

How Mrs Monkey Missed the Ark

Birdie Halleluyah!

The Other Goose

Goose in a Hole

Twinkles, Arthur and Puss

First published in hardback in Great Britain by HarperCollins Children's Books in 2009
First published in paperback in 2010

10 9 8 7 6 5 4 3 2 1
ISBN: 978-0-00-732113-1

HarperCollins Children's Books is a division of HarperCollins Publishers Ltd.
Text and illustrations copyright © Kerr-Kneale Productions Ltd 2009
The author/illustrator asserts the moral right to be identified as the author/illustrator of the work.
A CIP catalogue record for this title is available from the British Library.

Visit our website at: www.harpercollins.co.uk

Printed and bound in China

One Night
in the Zoo

Judith Kerr

HarperCollins *Children's Books*

One magical, moonlit night in the zoo

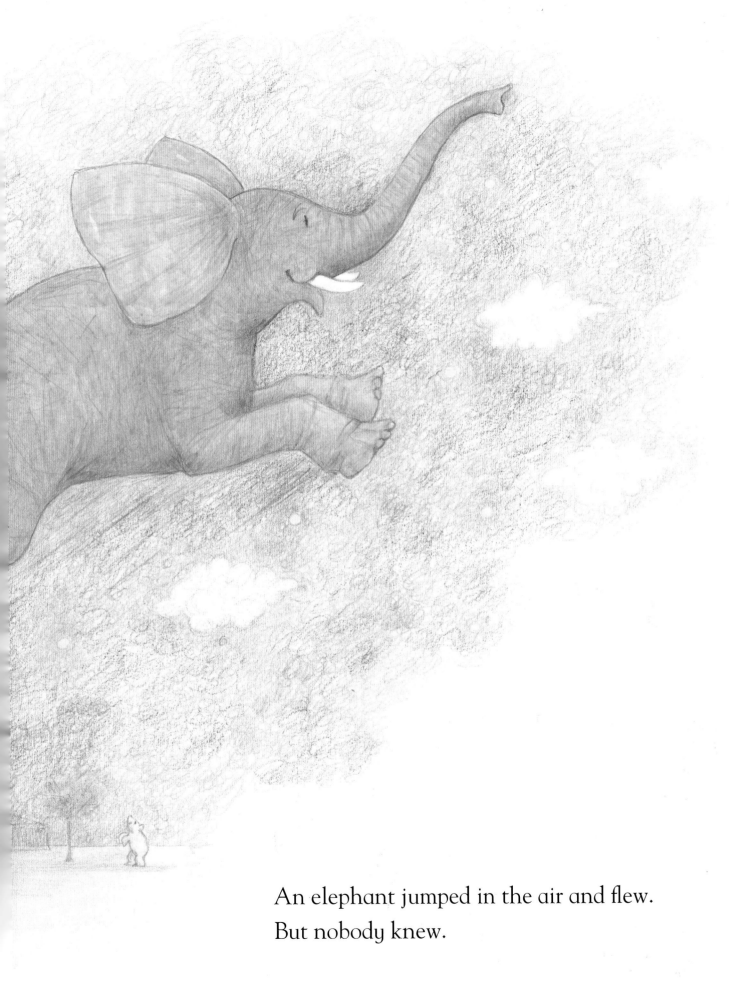

An elephant jumped in the air and flew.
But nobody knew.

Then a crocodile and a kangaroo
Set off on a bicycle made for two,

And three lions did tricks which astonished a gnu.
But nobody knew.

Four bears cooked a squid and squidgeberry stew

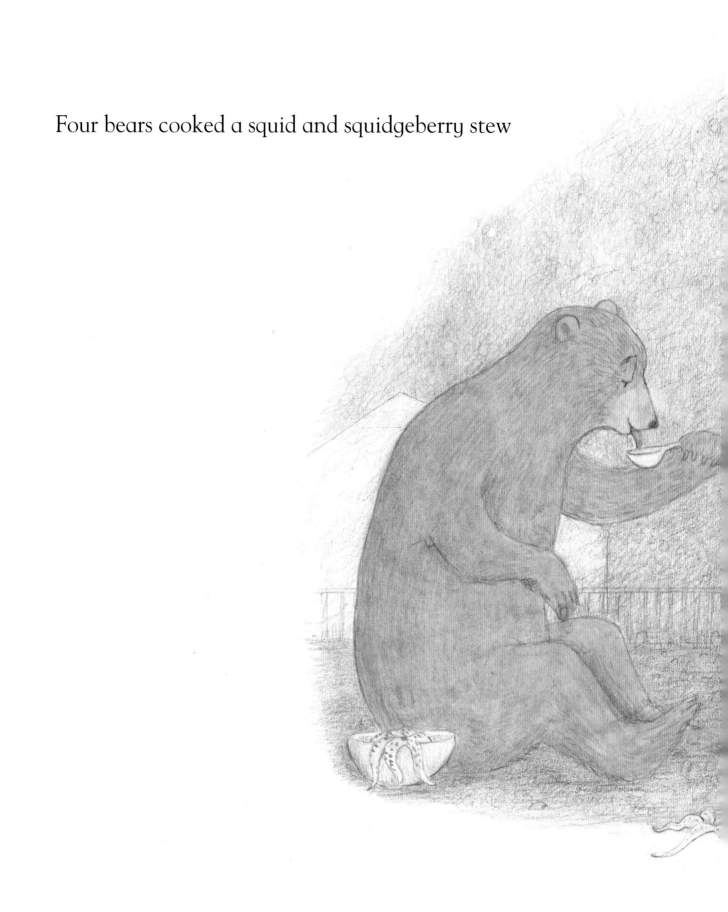

Which turned five flamingos
from pink to blue.

Six rabbits climbed a giraffe for the view.
But nobody knew.

Seven tigers sneezed: Atchoo! Atchoo!
Atchoo! Atchoo! Atchoo! Atchoo!
ATCHOO! And their seven sneezes blew
The feathers off a cockatoo.

Eight monkeys stuck them back with glue.
But nobody knew.

Then in the sky a pinkish hue
Broke through the dark, and as it grew
Nine owls cried, "Woo! Terwitterwoo!
The night is fading! Quickly! Shoo!
Back in your cages, all of you!"

The sun got up. The keeper, too.
Ten cocks crowed, "Cockadoodledoo!
He's coming! Quick! He's almost due!"

The keeper and his trusty crew
Found all the animals back on view
(excepting only one or two).

"They look so tired," he said. "All through
That moonlit night what *did* they do?"
But nobody knew…

…except you!

And here they are again.